# The
# Treasure Haunt

Find out more spooky secrets about

# Ghostville Elementary®

# Ghostville Elementary®

# The Treasure Haunt

by Marcia Thornton Jones
and
Debbie Dadey

illustrated by Guy Francis

A
**LITTLE APPLE**
PAPERBACK

## SCHOLASTIC INC.

New York   Toronto   London   Auckland   Sydney
Mexico City   New Delhi   Hong Kong   Buenos Aires

*For Shirlee Holloway — a real treasure!*
*— MTJ*

*For Eric, Nathan, Becky, and Alex —*
*my true treasures!*
*— DD*

No part of this publication may be reproduced, stored in a retrieval system, or transmitted in any form or by any means, electronic, mechanical, photocopying, recording, or otherwise, without written permission of the publisher. For information regarding permission, write to Scholastic Inc., Attention: Permissions Department, 557 Broadway, New York, NY 10012.

ISBN 0-439-67810-2

12 11 10 9 8 7 6 5 4 3 2 1         5 6 7 8 9 10/0

Printed in the U.S.A.         40
First printing, March 2005

# Contents

# THE LEGEND

*Sleepy Hollow Elementary School's*
*Online Newspaper*

**This Just In: Read-a-Thon might
be a nightmare!**

Breaking News: Can you believe the Mayor wants us to spend the night at school just so we can read? I bet we won't see *him* down in the creepy basement of Sleepy Hollow Elementary School when the clock strikes midnight. Only the third graders are crazy enough to do that. I wonder if they'll make it through the night? This could be one spooky sleepover. . . .

Stay tuned for more breaking news.


Your friendly fifth-grade reporter,
Justin Thyme

# The
# Treasure Haunt

# 1
# Ghost Time

"What are *you* doing here?" Ozzy asked. "It's Friday night. Friday the thirteenth, to be exact." He stretched to the height of a giant and glared down at the three kids standing in the basement classroom. His ghostly form glittered green around the edges of his overalls.

Cassidy, Jeff, and Nina were the first kids to arrive for their school's all-night Read-a-Thon. Their teacher, Mr. Morton, was in the hallway, signing in students and reassuring parents. The kids carried backpacks full of books, sleeping bags, pillows, and Jeff even had a little tent. Ghosts like Ozzy didn't scare them, at least not much.

Ever since they could remember, other kids had told ghost stories about the

boarded-up basement of their school. Most people believed the stories were nothing but legends made up to scare kids. Not Nina, Jeff, and Cassidy. They knew the tales were true. For some reason, the ghosts let themselves be seen and heard almost daily by the three friends. Ozzy was only one of many ghosts living in their third-grade classroom.

"We're having a reading party," Nina said politely. Her black hair was pulled back in a ponytail. She put a stack of library books on her desk.

"Party?" The question came from the shadows in one corner of the room. The air thickened and a green mist swirled until it took shape. Sadie wasn't exactly the happiest ghost in the basement, but she did try to be friendly. "I like birthday parties," Sadie said, smoothing her tattered dress and stringy hair.

"It's not a 'happy birthday' kind of party," Cassidy explained.

"It's a Read-a-Thon," Jeff said, dropping his tent onto the classroom floor with a thud.

"Every classroom in Sleepy Hollow is having a contest to see who can read the most books," Nina told the ghosts. "The winning classroom gets a brand-new computer."

Cassidy nodded. "It will have all the latest features." She started listing gadgets so fast her face turned red from lack of air.

Ozzy tapped his foot on the floor. Well, at least he tried to, but his foot sank into the tiles. "How long is this reading thing going to last?" he asked.

"All night!" Jeff said. "It's a sleepover."

Sadie turned from dull green to pale pink when she smiled. "Sleepovers are fun," she told her ghost friends. "At Nina's sleepover party, we danced to music." Sadie had followed Nina home on the night of her party.

"Becky wants to learn how to dance," Ozzy said. Cassidy looked around, expecting Ozzy's little sister to appear. She didn't, but another ghost, named Calliope, did. Calliope had followed them to school from an old mansion in town called the Blackburn Estate.

"And we painted our nails," Sadie went on.

"I've heard of painting fences, but I've never heard of painting nails," Ozzy said.

"Not everyone paints their nails," Jeff said with a smile. "Kids tell stories during

sleepovers, too. Ghost stories." Jeff loved watching scary shows on TV. In fact, some day he wanted to make his own movies.

Cassidy put her hands on her hips. "No, no, no!" she said. "We won't be doing any of those things. This isn't *that* kind of sleepover."

"Then what kind is it?" Sadie asked, the smile melting from her face as her skin went back to the color of wilted spinach and she slowly sank to the top of a desk.

"I know what kind it is," Ozzy interrupted. "It's the kind I don't like! It's bad enough that we have to share our room with you during the day," he said. "But nighttime is ghost time!"

Cassidy stuck out her chin. "Well, too bad. This is our classroom, too, and there isn't anything you can do about it."

"Shhh!" Jeff warned. But he was too late.

Ozzy's face turned the color of a forest fire and his eyes glowed orange.

Nina whimpered. Cassidy gasped. Jeff pulled his friends away. "Watch out!" he shouted.

# 2
# Burning

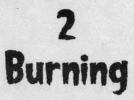

Ozzy loomed over the three kids, but he didn't get a chance to say a word. Just then, the hallway echoed with a stampede of sneakers. The ghosts scattered like gnats in the air.

"This is the Mayor's worst idea yet," Andrew complained, and threw a green sleeping bag beside his desk. "It's bad enough we have to go to school during the day, but spending the night here is just stupid."

"I think it's a great idea," Cassidy told him. "Our classroom could win the best computer ever made. You'd better get over your complaining and start reading. I don't see any stickers by your name."

Cassidy pointed to the poster behind

their teacher's desk. Cassidy's name had ten stickers next to it, one for each book she had read. Jeff and Nina each had eight. Carla and Darla had the most, with fifteen stickers each. There wasn't a single star next to Andrew's name.

"It would be nice if every class could get a new computer," Nina said as she set her backpack and sleeping bag next to her desk.

Andrew dumped his backpack on the floor as more kids filed into the room. "I think it would be nice if every classroom got boarded up and we never had to go to school again," Andrew told her.

Carla and her twin sister, Darla, skipped into the room. Carla stopped when she heard Andrew and nodded. "This room used to be . . ."

". . . boarded up," Darla finished. "But that's when people thought . . ."

". . . it was haunted," Carla said.

"Nobody believes those silly stories," Andrew said. "Do they?"

Nina and Cassidy stared at the air above Andrew. Ozzy floated there, plucking a stray hair out of Andrew's head.

"Ouch!" Andrew yelped and rubbed his head. He swirled around and glared at the twins. "Who did that?"

"Not me," Carla and Darla said together.

Cassidy giggled, but nobody heard her because their teacher bustled in, rubbing

his hands together. "Hurry," Mr. Morton said. "Push the desks out of the way and then find a space to read and sleep. We'll have pizza in an hour."

"Head for the back," Cassidy told Nina and Jeff after they scooted their desks against the wall. "Before Andrew beats us."

Jeff hurried to the back of the room and set up a small pup tent. Jeff stuck his head out of the tent. Cassidy and Nina put their bags beside Jeff's tent. The class settled in for a long night of reading. Everyone, of course, except the ghosts. Especially Ozzy.

The longer Ozzy watched, the more steamed up he got about the kids invading the classroom at night. Smoke started coming out of his nose and ears. Huge clouds of it seeped out of his head.

Carla stopped fluffing her pillow to sniff. "Call 911! Something . . ."

". . . is burning!" Darla yelled.

# 3
# Snake Attack

"Calm down," Mr. Morton told the class. "I'm sure everything is fine. Keep reading while I check it out."

When Mr. Morton stepped out into the hallway, Andrew tossed a paper wad at Carla.

Carla gave him a dirty look. "Just wait until . . ."

". . . Mr. Morton gets back," Darla finished for her.

Andrew hopped up from his sleeping bag and put his hands on his hips. "Just wait until Mr. Morton gets back," he said in a whiny voice. He stuck his nose in the air and wiggled his hips.

Cassidy didn't like Andrew's teasing, but she couldn't help smiling at the silly way he jiggled his hips.

Not Ozzy. He didn't like Andrew getting all the attention. Ozzy stopped steaming and dived right into Andrew's sleeping bag.

Cassidy gasped. What was Ozzy up to? She hoped she was the only one who noticed that Andrew's sleeping bag wiggled as if a big snake were inside.

"Everything's fine," Mr. Morton said as he hurried back to his desk. "That smell must have been from a big truck passing by the school. Let's get back to reading."

Mr. Morton sat at his desk and opened a fat book about dinosaurs. He didn't even notice Carla's hand in the air. Carla sighed and opened her book, *The Slime Wars*. Every once in a while she giggled, but everyone else silently read their books. Everyone except Andrew.

Andrew asked to go to the bathroom. Then he asked to get a drink. Finally, he asked to sharpen his pencil. "No," said Mr. Morton. "No. *No. NO!* Get in your sleeping bag and read."

"Sheesh, you don't have to get all mad." Andrew stomped over to his sleeping bag and scooted inside. Cassidy held her breath, hoping Ozzy had oozed back out. He hadn't.

The minute Andrew's legs hit the bottom of the bag, he screamed and shot out like a rocket. "Help!" he yelled. "Someone put a snake inside my bag."

Every girl and most of the boys

screamed and hopped up onto chairs.
Andrew stomped up and down on his
sleeping bag and pointed to Carla and
Darla.

"They did it!" he shouted.

# 4
# Vampire Bats

Carla shook her finger at Andrew. "We didn't touch . . ."

". . . your sleeping bag," finished Darla.

"I'm sure it was nothing," Mr. Morton said, but he picked up Andrew's sleeping bag and held it far away from his body. The whole class gulped as Mr. Morton pulled it open. Darla whimpered when their teacher stuck his head inside the bag.

Mr. Morton pulled his head out, frowned, and turned the bag inside out. Only Cassidy, Jeff, and Nina saw the ghost tumble from the bag. "Nothing," Mr. Morton snapped. "There is nothing in here but a little bit of lint."

"Something bit me!" Andrew insisted. Mr. Morton might have believed Barbara

or Allison, who never caused any trouble. But Andrew made it his business to get into mischief.

"No more interruptions. I am at a good part in my book. I want quiet!" Mr. Morton sat in his chair with a thud and opened his big blue book.

Everyone else hopped off their chairs and peeked inside their bags before snuggling in again. Just as Cassidy got interested in her story, she heard a jingling — or maybe it was a jangling — in the hallway.

The classroom door squeaked open. A huge shadow loomed in the doorway. Olivia, the school janitor, popped into the classroom. "I heard some screaming," she said. "Everything all right in here?"

Mr. Morton nodded. "Just a bit of Friday the thirteenth jitters."

"I understand completely," Olivia said with a smile. She was known for taking care of lost or hurt pets. She held up her arm. A tiny black bat hung upside down from her finger. "Don't be surprised if Bernie keeps you up tonight," Olivia warned. "Bats are nocturnal. Nighttime is their time. You can't blame a bat for liking the dark, just like you can't blame a cat for having whiskers. Remember that."

"It's odd how Olivia is always here," Nina remarked as Olivia closed the door with a click. Or maybe it was a clack.

"I think it's weird having a bat for a pet," Cassidy whispered. Something

about having a bat in the school gave her the shivers.

"I bet that's a vampire bat," Andrew said, and he wasn't whispering it, either. "The kind that turns innocent kids like Carla and Darla into blood-sucking vampire monsters. Oh, wait, I think that's already happened." Andrew snickered before Mr. Morton silenced him with a stern glance.

Andrew shut his mouth and pretended

to read, but Mr. Morton's warning didn't stop Ozzy.

Cassidy gasped when Ozzy appeared over Mr. Morton's head. The ghost's arms stretched into leathery wings and his teeth grew into fangs. Ozzy licked his lips and eyed Mr. Morton's neck. Then the ghost-turned-bat swooped straight toward Mr. Morton.

Cassidy screamed, "No!"

# 5
# Blood-sucking School Monsters

Mr. Morton stood up just as Ozzy made his move. The ghost ended up sinking his fangs into the back of Mr. Morton's chair. Mr. Morton hadn't seen a thing.

"That's *enough*. I am trying to read," Mr. Morton said. "*All* of you should be reading, too! Now stop this vampire nonsense and open your books!"

Ozzy floated away from the chair just as Mr. Morton plopped back down.

Cassidy and Nina crawled inside the tent with Jeff.

Jeff was propped up on a pillow, reading a book about movie monsters. Nina opened her biography about a famous soccer player from Brazil. Cassidy opened her book about legends and myths, but it was hard to read while Ozzy was doing his best to distract everyone. When he banged against the basement window, half the class screamed — and it wasn't just the girls, either.

"What if there really *are* vampire bats?" Nina whispered. "And what if they live down here in the basement?"

Jeff looked up from a picture of King Kong and grinned. "That would make a great show," he said softly. "I wonder if there's already one like it." He flipped to the back of the book and checked the index to see. "Nope. I don't see one. Maybe that could be my first big movie. I'd call it *The Blood-sucking School Monsters*."

Nina pulled her collar up to her chin. "Do you think it could really happen?"

"Vampire bats that suck people's blood are just stories told to scare kids," Cassidy said, but her voice shook when she said it. "Aren't they?"

"Well," Jeff said with a sly grin, "there really *are* vampire bats. But they don't turn people into monsters," he said.

"You're right," Cassidy said with a determined nod. "People have turned a little bit of truth into a horror story. Vampires are nothing more than legends, just like my book says."

"Pele is a legend, too," Nina said, tapping the cover of the biography she was reading. "A soccer legend. He can kick a ball clear to the moon."

"I think you're exaggerating just a bit," Jeff said.

"And that makes it a tall tale," Cassidy said. She knew about tall tales from her book, too. "And Jeff's monster stories are just folktales and fairy tales," she added.

Just then, the lights flickered twice and then went out. The room was plunged into total blackness. Cassidy was sure she heard Andrew scream louder than anybody.

Mr. Morton clicked on a flashlight.

"Calm down," he said. "There's nothing to worry about. I'm sure it's only a blown fuse." He rushed from the room and disappeared into the blackness of the basement hall to check.

"He left us . . ." Carla whimpered.

". . . alone in the dark," Darla added. After a bit of scrambling, several kids turned on their own flashlights.

Cassidy wasn't so sure their teacher was right about the fuse. She heard Ozzy laughing from someplace near the ceiling. Jeff found his flashlight and flicked it on. The light cast eerie shadows around the tent. Nina was sure she saw the outline of a ghost floating over them.

"I wish the ghosts in our room were nothing more than a story," Nina said with a shiver. Spending the night in a haunted classroom was not her idea of a good time.

"Ozzy's going to keep us from winning the computer," Cassidy whispered.

Jeff shrugged. "Remember what Olivia said about bats?" he asked. "We can't blame the ghosts for haunting, just like we can't blame her bat for being nocturnal. A ghost has to do what a ghost has to do!"

"And we have to do what we're supposed to do. Read," Nina said. "So forget about ghosts for now."

But Cassidy wasn't ready to forget.

29

"Ghost stories are legends," she said. "A legend is based on facts passed down from generation to generation."

"Is that how our online school paper, *The Legend*, got it's name?" Jeff said.

"Calling a newspaper *The Legend* wasn't a good idea," Cassidy said, "since legends are usually facts that have been stretched into exaggerated stories. Newspapers are supposed to be nothing but facts."

"Remember when we sneaked into *The Legend*'s office?" Nina asked. "We found that folder full of stories about local legends."

"I bet they'd be even more interesting than the ones in this book," Cassidy said.

Jeff grinned. His teeth glowed in the yellow beam of his flashlight. "I know how we can find out," he said.

"How?" Cassidy and Nina asked at the same time.

"Follow me," Jeff said. And then he slipped out of the tent.

# 6
# Amy Lou Marple

"Ouch," Carla squealed.

"You're stepping on us," Darla added.

"Sorry," Nina said as she followed Cassidy and Jeff across the room. The three friends tried to step carefully, but it was hard since all the kids were sprawled across the floor in sleeping bags. A few kids were still trying to read by the beams from their flashlights. Some kids talked, others started a pillow fight, and a few had the covers pulled over their heads.

Andrew hopped up, ready to join the three friends. "Where are you going?" he asked.

"Umm . . ." Cassidy said.

"Er . . ." Nina stammered.

Jeff was as quick with a fib as he was in a foot race. "We're going to get some cleaning supplies," he said. "There's some dirt on the floor near my tent. Do you want to help us clean the room?"

Andrew plopped back down on his sleeping bag. "No way," he said.

Cassidy, Jeff, and Nina followed the beam of Jeff's flashlight into the hall and up the narrow steps leading to the newer part of the school.

The electricity was out in the rest of the building, too. A cluster of teachers huddled near a closet, flipping circuit switches. At least the moon shining through the windows helped light the way as they headed toward *The Legend*'s office.

"Shhh," Jeff warned as they darted past open doorways.

The three friends hugged the wall near the principal's office and creeped along to the tiny newspaper office. When Jeff

slowly opened the door, the hinges creaked. The kids froze, waiting to see if Ms. Finkle would hurry from her office at the sound. When they were sure the coast was clear, they sneaked into *The Legend*'s office and gently closed the door.

Cassidy went straight to the file cabinet. "The folder of local legends was in the bottom drawer," she said as she pulled it open. Jeff shone the flashlight over her shoulder so she could find the right folder. When she did, she plopped it on the small desk nearby.

"See?" Nina said. "They're all legends about people right here in Sleepy Hollow."

"There's one about a catwoman who had real claws," Jeff said.

Nina saw another one. "Here's a story about somebody who could actually talk to animals."

Cassidy pulled another sheet from the folder. "This one's called *The Legend of Amy Lou Marple*."

"That's the one I saw before," Nina said.

Cassidy scanned the story. "According to the legend, Amy Lou was known as the bandit of Sleepy Hollow because she made off with the inheritance to a river-boat fortune."

"Calliope's parents owned a riverboat," Nina remembered.

"That means Amy Lou stole Calliope's fortune," Cassidy said.

"If I had a fortune, I could make all the movies I wanted," Jeff said. "What did the bandit of Sleepy Hollow do with the money she stole?"

"Amy Lou denied she even had it when the sheriff found her hiding at the schoolhouse," Cassidy read. "The bandit of Sleepy Hollow died before anyone could find where the loot was hidden."

"That would make a great movie," Jeff said.

"I thought you were going to make a movie about blood-sucking bats," Cassidy reminded him.

"Maybe I could make a movie about a blood-sucking bandit," Jeff thought out loud.

Nina wasn't sure she believed the legend. "Why would Amy Lou hide at school

when she could leave Sleepy Hollow and live like a queen with the fortune she stole?"

"Amy Lou," Jeff said slowly. "Amy Lou. Why does that name sound so familiar?"

And then Cassidy remembered. "I know!" Cassidy said. Unfortunately, she forgot to keep her voice quiet.

The kids heard the unmistakable sound of the principal's chair scooting across the floor.

*"Run!"* Jeff yelled.

He flung open the door and took off down the hall with his flashlight, leaving Cassidy and Nina totally in the dark.

# 7
# Mystery of the Missing Fortune

"I can't believe Jeff ditched us," Nina whimpered as a huge shadow filled the doorway.

"Don't worry," Cassidy whispered. "I have the perfect excuse."

Their principal, Ms. Finkle, flashed a light in their direction. "Who's in here?" The light glittered off Ms. Finkle's glasses and sparkled on her long, dagger-like fingernails.

"It's just us," Cassidy said bravely. "We're here to get a legend about our city to share with our class."

Nina nodded. "We found one about a bandit named Amy Lou Marple."

Ms. Finkle gasped and backed out of the room. "No," she muttered softly.

"Are you all right?" Cassidy asked.

Ms. Finkle cleared her throat. "Of course. Let me escort you back to your class. I'm sure we'll have the lights back on in no time. It isn't safe for you to be wandering around in the dark."

The girls followed the click-clack of Ms. Finkle's heels down the hallway, down the deep dark steps, and into the classroom. "Stay in your room until the lights come on," she ordered.

"Yes, ma'am," Nina said.

The girls crawled into Jeff's tent. "What took you guys so long?" he asked.

"We got caught by Ms. Finkle," Nina sputtered. "Thanks for leaving us in the dark."

Jeff's face turned red in the dim glow from his flashlight. "Sorry, I thought you were right behind me."

"Some friend you are," Cassidy said, "leaving us to face Ms. Finkle alone. But at least you didn't steal from your best friend."

"What are you talking about?" Jeff asked.

Cassidy pulled her friends close. "Amy Lou is the name of Calliope's best friend from over a hundred years ago."

"That's right," Nina sighed. "No wonder Calliope plays such sad music on her violin. Her best friend stole her money."

"Where did the legend say that Amy Lou was captured?" Cassidy asked slowly.

"The old schoolhouse," Nina told her.

Jeff shrugged. "So what?"

Cassidy, who planned to be an FBI computer spy someday, sat straight up, hitting her head on the top of Jeff's little tent. "We're in the basement of the oldest school in Sleepy Hollow."

"Do you think this could be the same school?" Nina asked.

"It has to be," Jeff said, jumping to his knees. "A hundred years ago there was only one school in Sleepy Hollow, and we're sitting in it."

Nina closed her book. "But the original Sleepy Hollow burned down. Even if Amy Lou hid her treasure here, it would've gone up in smoke with everything else."

Cassidy slumped back down on her sleeping bag. "You're right," she said. "Poor Calliope. First, her best friend steals her family's fortune. Then her money burns up."

Nina opened her book and settled into her sleeping bag. "We might as well keep reading. We don't have time to solve mysteries," she said.

Cassidy grinned. "If I find the treasure, we won't have to worry about winning that contest," she pointed out. "We'll be able to buy a computer for every kid in our class. Even the ghosts!"

The kids heard clapping outside when

the lights came back on. Cassidy peeked outside the tent. Mr. Morton stood in the middle of the room.

"Okay, kids. Back to reading," Mr. Morton said.

The kids read and ate pizza until it was late. Jeff noticed that Nate and Edgar had put up a ghost tent of their own inside an old pic-ture on the wall. Nate and Edgar were two ghosts that spent most of their time in a painting, writing stories. They had draped a blanket from the pic-ture's tree limbs, and their tent glowed as if they had a candle inside. Jeff hoped nobody bothered to look at the old pic-ture. The rest of the ghosts weren't as quiet. Ozzy rattled the windows and squeaked the door hinges. Sadie moaned and moaned. Calliope played screeching notes on her violin.

Finally, Mr. Morton cleared his throat. "Time to get some sleep," he said. "We'll be up bright and early to read more."

Some kids groaned and a few others went to the restroom, but in a little while everyone got quiet. Mr. Morton fell right to sleep. It was easy to tell because of his snoring.

Cassidy lay on top of her sleeping bag and wondered about the mystery. She smiled as she thought about all the computer gadgets she could buy with the treasure.

Ozzy, Sadie, and Becky glittered in different spots around the room. They tickled toes and dropped books, but most kids were so tired they fell asleep and didn't notice the noise.

Nina pulled her sleeping bag up to her chin. "How are we supposed to sleep with ghosts haunting our room?" she asked.

"Maybe they'll fall asleep soon," Cassidy said.

"No such luck," Jeff told her. "Everybody knows that ghosts can't rest until they've righted a wrong."

Cassidy sighed. She tossed and turned. She flipped her pillow. She kept thinking about the treasure. Something about the story wasn't right. If only Cassidy could figure it out!

# 8
# Silly Treasure Story

Cassidy, Jeff, and Nina awoke in the dead of night to a haunting melody playing on Calliope's violin. The tune was sad, and it didn't get any better when Calliope's ghost cat started singing along. Cocomo's wailing sounded like the wind howling through dead tree limbs.

Cassidy tossed. She turned. But the sad music kept her awake.

"Do you hear that?" Nina whispered in the night.

Cassidy nodded even though she knew Nina wouldn't be able to see her in the pitch-black of the classroom. "Poor Calliope," she said. "She sounds so sad."

"I bet that's why Calliope started haunting the Blackburn Estate," Jeff whispered. "And she can't rest until Amy Lou's wrong has been righted."

"I wish we could help Calliope," Nina said. She hated it when anybody was sad, even if it was a ghost.

"The only way we could do that is to find her treasure," Cassidy said.

"Treasure?" came a voice from right outside the tent. "What treasure?"

Andrew stuck his head inside the tent and grinned.

"You're supposed to be asleep," Cassidy told him.

"So are you," Andrew pointed out as he scooted inside the tent with the other three kids. "Besides," Andrew said, "who can sleep with Mr. Morton making all that racket?"

Mr. Morton's snoring hadn't stopped. It rumbled through the classroom like a saw cutting through wood. A feather from his pillow was stuck on his nose and it fluttered with every snore he made.

"Now, what's this about a treasure?" Andrew asked.

Jeff tried to make it sound like nothing. "We were just talking about that silly Blackburn treasure story," he said.

Andrew knew just what he meant. After all, his parents had bought the Blackburn Estate and he was looking

forward to living in the biggest mansion in the area. "That's no story," he said. "It's the truth. And I'm the one who's going to find that treasure."

"But it isn't yours," Nina said.

Andrew shook his head. "It is if I find it first," he said. "I'll be so rich that I'll come to school in a private helicopter."

"In your dreams," Cassidy said.

"Speaking of dreams, we'd better get back to sleep before Mr. Morton wakes up," Nina suggested.

Cassidy pushed Andrew back out of the tent. "Especially you," she said. "You're going to have a lot of reading to do in the morning if we're ever going to win that computer."

Mr. Morton snorted very loudly, and Andrew scooted the rest of the way out of the tent and wiggled into his sleeping bag.

Cassidy rubbed her eyes and put her spy brain to work. Amy Lou had been caught in the old schoolhouse. That had to mean

she hid the treasure before being caught by the sheriff. She knew from old pictures in the museum that the original school was simple. One room built over a cellar.

The cellar!

Cassidy jumped up out of her sleeping bag and knocked Jeff's whole tent down.

# 9
# Haunting Hour

Nina fought with the collapsed tent as if she were fighting a giant spider.

"Shhh," Cassidy warned as she slapped her hand over Nina's mouth. Jeff pulled off the tent and the three kids froze, waiting to see if anyone else in the room was awake.

Andrew mumbled something in his sleep about giant petunias, and Barbara flopped over in her sleeping bag. The rest of the class was quiet.

"What happened?" Nina hissed.

"I just figured out where Amy Lou hid the treasure," Cassidy said, "that's what happened! Follow me and I'll tell you all about it."

Nina followed Cassidy and Jeff. They made their way past the sleeping third

graders, making sure not to step on any fingers or toes. They paused and held their breaths when Mr. Morton stopped snoring. But then he snorted and started snoring again.

Once they were in the hall, Jeff turned to Cassidy. "What's going on?" he asked as she softly closed the classroom door.

The bells in the old church down the street struck twelve times.

"Midnight," Nina mumbled with a shiver. "The haunting hour."

"Don't worry about that. I've figured out where the treasure is," Cassidy whispered.

Jeff switched on his flashlight and stared in disbelief at Cassidy. "Where is it, then?" he asked.

"Well, I don't know exactly *where* it is, but I figured out it has to be somewhere right here in the basement of Ghostville Elementary," Cassidy told her friends.

Jeff shook his head. "Amy Lou Marple was caught in the *old* Sleepy Hollow Elementary — the one that burned down."

Cassidy nodded. "But there wouldn't be any place to hide a treasure in a one-room schoolhouse," she said, "except in the cellar. And the cellar didn't burn."

Nina gasped. "You could be right! If Amy Lou hid the treasure somewhere in the basement, it could still be here!"

"But where?" Cassidy asked.

"The desks, the chairs, the bookshelves. They've all been used a hundred times," Nina said.

"Everything," Jeff said, "except for one thing." Jeff flashed the weak beam of his flashlight down the hallway. It landed on an old cabinet that had been built into the walls of the basement. "That cabinet was here on the night Amy Lou was caught by the sheriff. It's the *only* thing that hasn't been used."

The kids had tried to look in the cabinet before but the ghosts wouldn't let them near it. "The treasure is in there," Cassidy said. "It's the only place it *can* be. Hurry, before the ghosts try to stop us again."

Cassidy, Jeff, and Nina sprinted down the hall toward the cabinet. Jeff reached it first. Just as he grabbed the old brass handle, Ozzy popped out of the wall. When he saw Jeff, he let out a scream. It wasn't just any scream, either. It was so loud it cracked the window at the other end of the hallway.

"Why are you here? Why are you in *my* hallway? This is our time. *Ghost time!*"

Ozzy's roar brought the other ghosts. Calliope oozed from under the crack of a door, followed by her ghostly cat, Cocomo. Cocomo's eyes glowed yellow and her black fur shimmered with green. She hissed at Jeff and swiped at his knee.

Jeff jumped back just in time. The cat's claws raked all the way through the

brick wall next to Jeff. He felt a breeze as cold as an icicle.

The air next to Ozzy glittered green as his little sister, Becky, took shape. "They're stealing!" she screeched.

"Noooooo," Sadie cried as she rose from the drain of the drinking fountain. "Stealing is wrong!"

"We're not stealing," Nina said. "We just wanted to find Calliope's long-lost treasure that Amy Lou stole from her."

"NOOOOOOOO! Stop them!" Calliope screamed, then she flew through the air straight for the kids.

The ghosts joined together, reaching out long ghostly fingers toward the kids.

Cassidy, Nina, and Jeff huddled together as the ghosts came closer and closer. They were trapped with nowhere to run.

# 10
# Vampire Bats and Insane Ghosts

Nina closed her eyes. Jeff held his breath. Cassidy felt like throwing up. She couldn't believe this was the end. The Sleepy Hollow newspaper would say three kids disappeared under mysterious circumstances during their Read-a-Thon. No one would know that ghosts got them.

Cassidy wasn't ready to give up. "No!" she yelled at the ghosts. "You can't keep me from getting that treasure!"

Ozzy twisted himself up like a chain and loomed over Cassidy. "Stealing is bad!"

"We weren't stealing!" Cassidy snorted back.

Just when all seemed lost, the kids heard a jingling — or maybe it was a jangling. Olivia, the school janitor, switched on the hall lights. She stood with her hands on her big hips and stared at the kids. A huge ring of keys hung from the side of her red overalls. "Why aren't you asleep?" she asked. "And what's going on out here?"

Ozzy, Becky, Sadie, Cocomo, and Calliope took one look at Olivia and disappeared with a big green *pop*.

Nina opened her eyes and said, "Ummm."

"We were just trying to win a computer," Cassidy said slowly. "We stayed up late to read. Yeah. That's it."

Olivia nodded. She knew how much Cassidy liked computers. "Those computers are marvelous things. But I don't see any here in the hallway," Olivia pointed out.

"We were getting a drink," Jeff said quickly.

Olivia pointed in the other direction. "The water fountain is over there."

Jeff's face turned red. "Oh, yeah. Thanks."

"I suppose it's easy to misunderstand what a person is doing," Olivia said. She looked up at the cobwebbed ceiling. "Keep an eye out for Bernie. He seems to be out and about."

Nina gulped and covered her neck with her hands. Bernie the bat could be

anywhere, ready to pounce on her. Just like the ghosts.

Olivia frowned at the kids and her long earrings jingled — or maybe they jangled. "You best get back in the classroom."

Olivia jingled and jangled down the hall. When she had disappeared around a corner, Nina squealed, "I'm going back to the classroom before a vampire bat or insane ghost gets me!"

Jeff nodded. "No treasure is worth all this. There's no telling what those ghosts might do."

But Cassidy stood her ground in the middle of the dark hallway. She shook her head. "We're not going anywhere!"

# 11
# Ghost Boogers

"We're going to get that treasure!" Cassidy snapped. She ran toward the hallway cabinet.

"No!" Nina shouted, but it was too late. The ghosts were already there. Ozzy popped up in front of Cassidy, shaped like a wooden door. Cassidy smashed into Ozzy face-first.

Cassidy fell to the floor in a daze. It felt like she had run into an iceberg. Her teeth chattered and her lips turned blue.

"Are you all right?" Nina asked, rushing to her friend's side.

"Ozzy is serious," Jeff said. "It takes a lot of concentration to become solid like that."

Cassidy shook her head. "He's not

going to stop me." She hopped up, ready to push Ozzy aside.

The minute Cassidy got up, Becky and Sadie appeared above her. The two ghosts reached long fingers up their noses and pulled out green ghost boogers. They sent them flying at Cassidy. Each ghost booger felt like a snowball splattering on her bare skin.

"Stop it!" Cassidy shrieked.

"It's not right to steal!" Sadie moaned as she threw another ghost booger at Cassidy.

Cassidy yanked open the cabinet, and Ozzy hit her full force. He puffed out his cheeks until they were the size of watermelons. Then he blew. Hard.

Cassidy flew to the ceiling and stayed there, bouncing in the air on Ozzy's breath.

Nina screamed when Jeff dived for Cassidy. Ozzy caught Jeff with his breath, too. Cassidy and Jeff both

bounced around in the air while Sadie and Becky bombarded them with boogers.

"Do something!" Cassidy yelled to Nina.

Nina dove behind Ozzy and landed right inside the cabinet on top of a pile of very old newspapers. She hit something hard. Thowing the papers aside, she found a wooden box big enough to hold a pair of tennis shoes. It was old, with fancy carvings. A brass latch locked it tight.

"I think I found it!" Nina sputtered as she stuck her head out of the cabinet. She held it out for the ghosts to see. "Now, leave them alone!"

All the ghosts stopped what they were doing to face Nina. When they did, Cassidy and Jeff dropped to the floor with a thud.

"Ouch," Jeff said when he landed on the floor.

"Ouch," they both said when Cassidy landed on Jeff.

Ozzy reached for the treasure box. "At last," he said. "After all these years, the treasure is mine."

"It's *not* yours," Cassidy said. "It's mine! I need it to buy computers for our classroom."

Nina shook her head. "It doesn't belong to either of you," she said. "If it's

really the legendary treasure, it belongs to Calliope. Amy Lou stole it from *her*."

Calliope pushed past Ozzy and the rest of the ghosts and came face-to-face with Nina. "You're wrong," she said. Her voice was low and she sounded like she was ready to cry. "They were all wrong. Amy Lou stole nothing from me. I gave her my family's fortune."

"Why would you give your best friend your family's money?" Cassidy asked.

Calliope seemed to shrink with every word she spoke. She turned the color of a rotten plum. "My uncle was a selfish man," she said. "He wanted that money for himself. Amy Lou agreed to hide it for me."

"So the legend is wrong," Nina said softly.

"Amy Lou was no bandit," Calliope said with a shake of her head. "She was my friend. My only friend. But I never told the truth. Until now."

"We'll rewrite the legend," Cassidy

said. "We'll let everyone know that Amy Lou didn't steal your money."

Calliope brightened and grew a little taller. "You will?"

"Of course," Nina said. "Now take this. It's rightfully yours."

Calliope looked at the box. "But what shall I do with it?"

Before anyone could answer, a loud voice echoed down the hallway.

"What are you children doing out here?" Mr. Morton asked.

It was as if a switch had been thrown. All the ghosts disappeared, leaving Jeff and Cassidy on the floor and Nina halfway inside the old cabinet, holding the wooden box.

Mr. Morton stomped down the hall. "Where did this come from?" he demanded as he reached for the box in Nina's hand. Nina was so surprised that she couldn't answer.

"You kids need to get back to sleep," Mr. Morton said. "I'll take care of this."

Cassidy really wanted to tell Mr. Morton the whole story, but just then a black shadow swooped down the hall and headed straight for their teacher.

# 12
# Secret Friend

"*AHHHHHHHH!*" Nina screamed so loudly, the cracked glass in the basement window rattled.

Cassidy ducked. Jeff dived for the floor.

Mr. Morton dropped the box and held his hands in front of his face as leathery wings flapped around his head.

"Bernie!" Olivia said as she stepped into the hallway. "What are you doing, scaring these poor people half out of their skins?"

Olivia jingled and jangled the rest of the way down the hall. She plucked the cap off her head and gently used it to scoop the flapping bat out of the air. "Poor thing," she said. "He's not used to having so much company at night. He's a bit out of sorts. All these kids, flipping the pages of their books until the wee hours of the morning, made him grumpy."

Mr. Morton straightened the glasses on his nose and took a breath. "That's all right. I understand about being nervous."

Olivia smiled. But then she caught sight of the box lying on the floor, and the smile disappeared from her face.

Olivia slowly bent down and picked up the box. "I've been hunting for this for years," she said.

Mr. Morton brushed off his hands. "The kids were doing a little late-night exploring and found it," he explained.

"Is that so?" Olivia said, looking at Cassidy, Jeff, and Nina. "Well, thanks for digging it up. I know just what to do with it."

With that, Olivia and Bernie disappeared down the hall and into Olivia's workshop.

\* \* \*

The next Monday, the kids met after school by the jungle gym. "I can't believe we lost the contest," Cassidy groaned. "It's all Andrew's fault. He didn't read a single book."

"Doesn't he know how much fun reading can be?" Nina asked.

Jeff shrugged and hopped onto the jungle gym. "A new computer would have been nice, but not as nice as having a treasure all to ourselves."

Cassidy sighed. "I wonder what Olivia did with Calliope's family fortune."

"We don't know for sure that was the missing treasure," Nina admitted. "Maybe it was just a box full of nuts and bolts."

Jeff jumped off the bar and pointed to the back of the school. "Who cares about nuts and bolts? Look at what just pulled up to the school!"

Cassidy and Nina turned to see a huge truck pull to a stop. COMPUTERS FOR SCHOOL USE was written in big letters

on the side. Two men jumped down from the truck and started unloading box after box after box. One of the men stopped long enough to answer Cassidy when she politely asked what they were doing.

"Seems like you have a secret friend," he told her. "Somebody decided to buy a computer for every classroom at Sleepy Hollow."

"You don't suppose Olivia used the treasure money to buy computers, do you?" Jeff asked slowly as the men went back to work.

"If she did, I hope Calliope doesn't mind sharing it with us," Nina said.

"We'll share our school with her," Cassidy said, "and she'll share her computers with us."

"Does that mean we'll all live happily ever after, just like in the movies?" Jeff asked.

Nina shrugged. With a basement full of ghosts, happily ever after didn't sound too likely. "I hope so," she said softly. "I really, really hope so."

# About the Authors

Marcia Thornton Jones and Debbie Dadey got into the *spirit* of writing when they worked together at the same school in Lexington, Kentucky. Since then, Debbie has *haunted* several states. She currently *haunts* Ft. Collins, CO, with her three children, two dogs, and husband. Marcia remains in Lexington, KY, where she lives with her husband and two cats. Debbie and Marcia have fun with spooky stories. They have scared themselves silly with *The Adventures of the Bailey School Kids* and *The Bailey City Monsters* series.

**Ready for more spooky fun?**
**Then take a sneak peek at the next**

# Ghostville Elementary®

## #12 Frights! Camera! Action!

Hollywood is coming to Sleepy Hollow! A big-time director wants to film a monster movie in the third graders' basement classroom. Jeff can't wait to see how a real scary movie is made. He wants to help out with costumes, props, and special effects. But the classroom ghosts want to help out, too. And that could be a nightmare!

Creepy, weird, wacky, and
funny things happen to
The Bailey School Kids!™
Collect and read them all!

The Adventures of
THE
BAILEY SCHOOL
KIDS®

| | | | | |
|---|---|---|---|---|
| ❑ 0-590-43411-X | #1 | Vampires Don't Wear Polka Dots | ........................ | $3.99 US |
| ❑ 0-590-44061-6 | #2 | Werewolves Don't Go to Summer Camp | ................. | $3.99 US |
| ❑ 0-590-44477-8 | #3 | Santa Claus Doesn't Mop Floors | ..................... | $3.99 US |
| ❑ 0-590-44822-6 | #4 | Leprechauns Don't Play Basketball | .................... | $3.99 US |
| ❑ 0-590-45854-X | #5 | Ghosts Don't Eat Potato Chips | ...................... | $3.99 US |
| ❑ 0-590-47071-X | #6 | Frankenstein Doesn't Plant Petunias | .................. | $3.99 US |
| ❑ 0-590-47070-1 | #7 | Aliens Don't Wear Braces | ........................... | $3.99 US |
| ❑ 0-590-47297-6 | #8 | Genies Don't Ride Bicycles | .......................... | $3.99 US |
| ❑ 0-590-47298-4 | #9 | Pirates Don't Wear Pink Sunglasses | .................. | $3.99 US |
| ❑ 0-590-48112-6 | #10 | Witches Don't Do Backflips | .......................... | $3.99 US |
| ❑ 0-590-48113-4 | #11 | Skeletons Don't Play Tubas | .......................... | $3.99 US |
| ❑ 0-590-48114-2 | #12 | Cupid Doesn't Flip Hamburgers | ...................... | $3.99 US |
| ❑ 0-590-48115-0 | #13 | Gremlins Don't Chew Bubble Gum | ................... | $3.99 US |
| ❑ 0-590-22635-5 | #14 | Monsters Don't Scuba Dive | .......................... | $3.99 US |
| ❑ 0-590-22636-3 | #15 | Zombies Don't Play Soccer | .......................... | $3.99 US |
| ❑ 0-590-22638-X | #16 | Dracula Doesn't Drink Lemonade | .................... | $3.99 US |
| ❑ 0-590-22637-1 | #17 | Elves Don't Wear Hard Hats | ........................ | $3.99 US |
| ❑ 0-590-50960-8 | #18 | Martians Don't Take Temperatures | ................... | $3.99 US |
| ❑ 0-590-50961-6 | #19 | Gargoyles Don't Drive School Buses | ................. | $3.99 US |
| ❑ 0-590-50962-4 | #20 | Wizards Don't Need Computers | ...................... | $3.99 US |
| ❑ 0-590-22639-8 | #21 | Mummies Don't Coach Softball | ...................... | $3.99 US |
| ❑ 0-590-84886-0 | #22 | Cyclops Doesn't Roller-Skate | ........................ | $3.99 US |
| ❑ 0-590-84902-6 | #23 | Angels Don't Know Karate | .......................... | $3.99 US |
| ❑ 0-590-84904-2 | #24 | Dragons Don't Cook Pizza | .......................... | $3.99 US |
| ❑ 0-590-84905-0 | #25 | Bigfoot Doesn't Square Dance | ....................... | $3.99 US |
| ❑ 0-590-84906-9 | #26 | Mermaids Don't Run Track | .......................... | $3.99 US |
| ❑ 0-590-25701-3 | #27 | Bogeymen Don't Play Football | ....................... | $3.99 US |
| ❑ 0-590-25783-8 | #28 | Unicorns Don't Give Sleigh Rides | .................... | $3.99 US |
| ❑ 0-590-25804-4 | #29 | Knights Don't Teach Piano | .......................... | $3.99 US |
| ❑ 0-590-25809-5 | #30 | Hercules Doesn't Pull Teeth | ......................... | $3.99 US |
| ❑ 0-590-25819-2 | #31 | Ghouls Don't Scoop Ice Cream | ...................... | $3.99 US |
| ❑ 0-590-18982-4 | #32 | Phantoms Don't Drive Sports Cars | ................... | $3.99 US |
| ❑ 0-590-18983-2 | #33 | Giants Don't Go Snowboarding | ...................... | $3.99 US |
| ❑ 0-590-18984-0 | #34 | Frankenstein Doesn't Slam Hockey Pucks | .............. | $3.99 US |
| ❑ 0-590-18985-9 | #35 | Trolls Don't Ride Roller Coasters | .................... | $3.99 US |
| ❑ 0-590-18986-7 | #36 | Wolfmen Don't Hula Dance | ......................... | $3.99 US |

The Adventures of **THE BAILEY SCHOOL KIDS**®

❏ 0-439-04397-2 #37 Goblins Don't Play Video Games .......................... $3.99 US
❏ 0-439-04398-0 #38 Ninjas Don't Bake Pumpkin Pie .......................... $3.99 US
❏ 0-439-04399-9 #39 Dracula Doesn't Rock and Roll .......................... $3.99 US
❏ 0-439-04401-4 #40 Sea Monsters Don't Ride Motorcycles .................... $3.99 US
❏ 0-439-04400-6 #41 The Bride of Frankenstein Doesn't Bake Cookies............ $3.99 US
❏ 0-439-21582-X #42 Robots Don't Catch Chicken Pox ........................ $3.99 US
❏ 0-439-21583-8 #43 Vikings Don't Wear Wrestling Belts ..................... $3.99 US
❏ 0-439-21584-6 #44 Ghosts Don't Rope Wild Horses ......................... $3.99 US
❏ 0-439-36803-0 #45 Wizards Don't Wear Graduation Gowns ................... $3.99 US
❏ 0-439-36805-7 #46 Sea Serpents Don't Juggle Water Balloons................. $3.99 US
❏ 0-439-55999-5 #47 Frankenstein Doesn't Start Food Fights .................. $3.99 US
❏ 0-439-56000-4 #48 Dracula Doesn't Play Kickball .......................... $3.99 US
❏ 0-439-65036-4 #49 Werewolves Don't Run For President ..................... $3.99 US
❏ 0-439-65037-2 #50 The Abominable Snowman Doesn't Roast Marshmallows........ $3.99 US

❏ 0-439-40831-8    Bailey School Kids Holiday Special:
                   Aliens Don't Carve Jack-o'-lanterns ........................ $3.99 US
❏ 0-439-40832-6    Bailey School Kids Holiday Special:
                   Mrs. Claus Doesn't Climb Telephone Poles .................. $3.99 US
❏ 0-439-33338-5    Bailey School Kids Thanksgiving Special:
                   Swamp Monsters Don't Chase Wild Turkeys ................. $3.99 US
❏ 0-439-40834-2    Bailey School Kids Holiday Special:
                   Ogres Don't Hunt Easter Eggs ............................ $3.99 US
❏ 0-439-40833-4    Bailey School Kids Holiday Special:
                   Leprechauns Don't Play Fetch ............................ $3.99 US

**Available wherever you buy books, or use this order form.**

### Scholastic Inc., P.O. Box 7502, Jefferson City, MO 65102

Please send me the books I have checked above. I am enclosing $_____ (please add $2.00 to cover shipping and handling). Send check or money order — no cash or C.O.D.s please.

Name ——————————————————————————————

Address —————————————————————————————

City ————————————————— State/Zip ————————————

Please allow four to six weeks for delivery. Offer good in the U.S. only. Sorry, mail orders are not available to residents of Canada. Prices subject to change.

# MORE SERIES YOU'LL LOVE

**J**igsaw and his partner, Mila, know that mysteries are like jigsaw puzzles—you've got to look at all the pieces to solve the case!

## THE SECRETS OF DROON

Under the stairs a magical world awaits you.

**Hey L'il D!**

**L**'il Dobber has two things with him at all times—his basketball and his friends. Together, they are a great team. And they are always looking for adventure and fun—on and off the b'ball court!

# GET READY FOR MONSTER-SIZED LAUGHS!

**THE TEACHERS FROM THE BLACK LAGOON ARE A SCARY BUNCH, BUT WHEN YOU MEET THEM YOU WON'T KNOW WHETHER TO SHIVER...OR GIGGLE YOURSELF SILLY.**

- ☐ 0-439-42927-7 **Black Lagoon Adventures #1: The Class Trip From the Black Lagoon**   $3.99 US
- ☐ 0-439-43894-2 **Black Lagoon Adventures #2: The Talent Show From the Black Lagoon**   $3.99 US
- ☐ 0-439-55716-X **Black Lagoon Adventures #3: The Class Election From the Black Lagoon**   $3.99 US
- ☐ 0-439-55717-8 **Black Lagoon Adventures #4: The Science Fair From the Black Lagoon**   $3.99 US

**AVAILABLE WHEREVER YOU BUY BOOKS, OR USE THIS ORDER FORM.**

**www.scholastic.com**

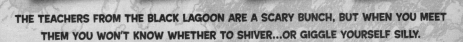

**SCHOLASTIC**